HUFF and PUFF on THANKSGIVING

Warren Publishing House, Inc.

Warren Publishing House, Inc., P.O. Box 2250, Everett, WA 98203, 1-800-334-4769.

Printed in Hong Kong by Mandarin Offset.
First Edition   10 9 8 7 6 5 4 3 2 1

Cataloging-in-Publication Information

Warren, Jean
      Huff and Puff on Thanksgiving/by Jean Warren; illustrated by Molly Piper; activity illustrations by Marion Ekberg. — 1st ed. — Everett, WA: Warren Publishing House, Inc., © 1993.

32 p.:ill.

Activity suggestions included (p. 20-32).

      Summary: Huff and Puff, two lovable, child-like cloud characters, celebrate Thanksgiving with their family and human friends below.

1. Creative activities. 2. Holidays—Handbooks, manuals, etc. 3. Thanksgiving—Handbooks, manuals, etc.

I. Piper, Molly   II. Ekberg, Marion   III. Title

93-13545
ISBN 0-911019-70-7

745
(E)

Warren Publishing House, Inc. would like to acknowledge the following activity contributors:

Betty Ruth Baker, Waco, TX
Judy Hall, Wytheville, VA
Becky Valenick, Rockford, IL
Margery A. Kranyik, Hyde Park, MA
Cathy B. Griffin, Plainsboro, NJ

HUFF and PUFF on THANKSGIVING
By Jean Warren

Illustrated by Molly Piper
Activity Illustrations by Marion Ekberg

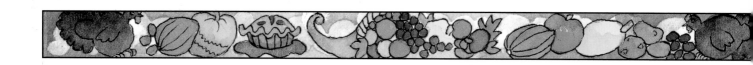

Huff and Puff were happy,
It was Thanksgiving Day.
Their relatives were coming
From near and far away.

They cleaned their rooms all morning,
Then swept across the sky.
They showered off each other,
Then rolled around to dry.

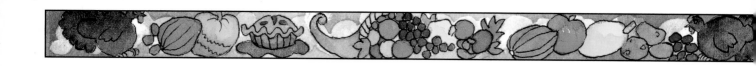

They puffed up like two turkeys
And waddled 'round the sky,
Greeting everybody
With a gobble-gobble "Hi."

First, with the turkey,
Came great big Grandpa Gruff.
Then, loaded down with pies,
Came sweet old Grandma Muff.

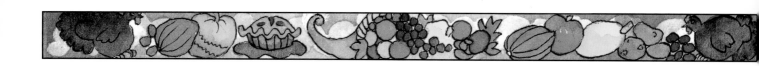

Next, carrying two baskets,
Came jolly Uncle Stuff,
Followed by the happy face
Of their Aunty Fluff.

Then came all the cousins,
Including Baby Buff.
Last there came the monsters,
Cousins Ruff and Tuff.

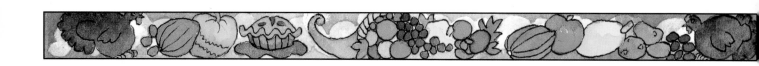

The party was beginning!
Huff and Puff were glad to see
So many smiling faces
In their great big family.

At last, the food was ready
And they gathered 'round to say,
"Thank you for our blessings
On this very special day."

The dinner was delicious
And worth the long, long wait,
And everyone, as usual,
Ate and ate and ate.

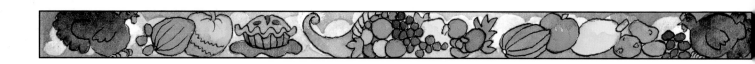

When all the bowls were empty,
And all the dishes done,
The family went outside
To watch the setting sun.

Then Grandpa grabbed his fiddle
And played a lively tune.
Soon everyone was dancing
'Round and 'round the moon.

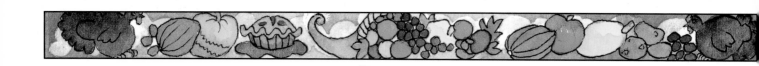

Grandma sang a simple song
She learned when she was young.
She taught them all the words,
And how the song was sung.

The cousins got together
And planned a funny skit.
Soon everyone was laughing,
It was a great big hit.

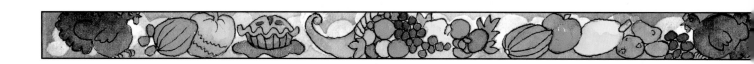

Too soon the day was over,
And they all said good-bye
To Huff and Puff who watched them,
As they rolled across the sky.

"What a happy celebration,"
Huff and Puff were heard to say,
"Don't you wish that every day
Could be Thanksgiving Day?"

Thanksgiving
Fun

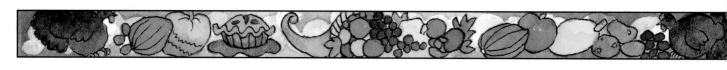

May Peace Be Everywhere

Sung to: "The Battle Hymn of the Republic"

I love to see the faces of my
Friends and family,
I love to sit down with them and
Eat pie and turkey.
I love to get together on this
Extra-special day,
A time to share and care.

Happy, happy Thanksgiving,
Happy, happy Thanksgiving,
Happy, happy Thanksgiving.
May peace be everywhere!

Jean Warren

Smells Like Thanksgiving

Sung to: "Frere Jacques"

Smells like Thanksgiving,
Smells like Thanksgiving,
Mmmm so good,
Mmmm so good.
I can smell the turkey,
I can smell the pies,
Mmmm so good,
Mmmm so good.

Jean Warren

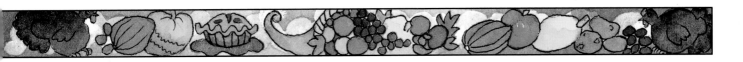

The Pilgrims Are Coming

Sung to: "When Johnny Comes Marching Home"

The Pilgrims are coming to celebrate,
Hurray! Hurray!
The Pilgrims are coming to celebrate
Thanksgiving Day.
The Pilgrims are coming
So don't be late,
We'll eat and dance to celebrate.
And we'll all be glad, so
Hurry and don't be late!

The Indians are coming to celebrate,
Hurray! Hurray!
The Indians are coming to celebrate
Thanksgiving Day.
The Indians are coming
So don't be late,
We'll eat and dance to celebrate.
And we'll all be glad, so
Hurry and don't be late!

Jean Warren

Thanksgiving Day

Sung to: "Old MacDonald"

Thanksgiving Day will soon be here,
Let us now give thanks.
For the blessings of the year.
Let us now give thanks,
With a thankful heart,
With a thankful heart.
On this day, we'll stop to say,
"For the blessings of the year,
Let us now give thanks."

Betty Ruth Baker

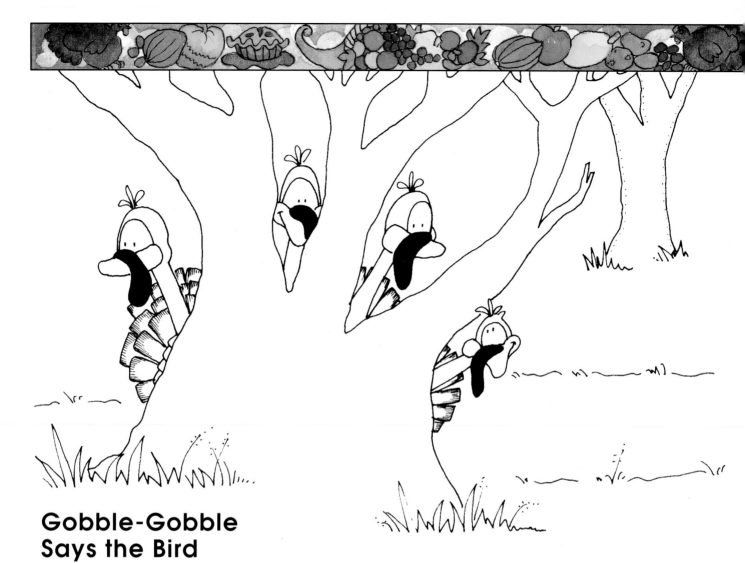

Gobble-Gobble
Says the Bird

Sung to: "If You're Happy and
You Know It"

Gobble-gobble, gobble-gobble,

Says the bird,

Gobble-gobble, gobble-gobble,

Says the bird.

Mr. Turkey gobble-gobbles

And his feet go wobble-wobble.

Gobble-gobble, gobble-gobble,

Says the bird.

Becky Valenick

Turkey, Turkey

Sung to: "Twinkle, Twinkle,
Little Star"

Turkey, Turkey, look at you,

Please be careful what you do.

Thanksgiving Day is almost here,

We eat turkey every year.

Go and hide out in the woods,

We'll eat pizza, as we should!

Judy Hall

There's a Big Fat Turkey
Sung to: "Little White Duck"

There's a big, fat turkey
Down on the farm.
A big, fat turkey
Who stays away from harm.
He's always gone on
Thanksgiving Day,
For some odd reason
He just runs away.
There's a big, fat turkey
Down on the farm.
Gobble, gobble, gobble.

Jean Warren

Mr. Turkey
Sung to: "Frere Jaques"

Mr. Turkey,
Mr. Turkey,
Run away,
Run away.
If you are not careful,
You will be a mouthful,
Thanksgiving Day,
Thanksgiving Day.

Margery A. Kranyik

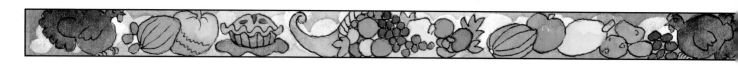

Colorful-Corn Napkin Rings

1. Cut a cardboard toilet-tissue tube into four rings.

2. Brush glue all over the rings.

3. Roll the rings in Indian-corn kernels.

4. Let the napkin rings dry.

Get "corny" with these fun and easy napkin rings!

You Will Need

scissors • a cardboard toilet-tissue tube • a paintbrush • glue • Indian-corn kernels

For More Fun

• Use all kinds of other materials to decorate your napkin rings, such as small squares of colored construction paper, scraps of yarn and fabric, glitter, buttons, and so on.

Hand-Print Turkey Card

Greet your friends and family with an original turkey card!

1. Fold a piece of white paper in half.

2. Paint the inside of one of your hands and thumb brown.

3. On that same hand, paint the insides of your fingers red, yellow, and orange.

4. Spread your fingers and thumb apart and press your hand on the front of your folded paper to make a hand-print turkey body.

You Will Need

a piece of white paper • a paintbrush • brown, red, yellow, and orange paint • felt-tip markers

5. Paint one of your fingertips red and press it under your turkey's chin to make a red wattle.

6. When the paint is dry, use felt-tip markers to add eyes, a beak, and legs to your turkey.

7. Write a simple Thanksgiving greeting, like the poem below, inside your card.

For More Fun

• Write the following poem inside your card.

This isn't just a turkey,
As anyone can see.
I made it with my hand,
Which is a part of me!
It comes with lots of love,
Specially to say —
I hope you have a very happy
Thanksgiving Day!

Turkey Puppet

1.

2.

3-4.

Make this turkey puppet to help you celebrate Thanksgiving!

1. Fold a piece of brown paper as shown in the pictures above.

2. Use felt-tip markers to draw eyes on the puppet.

3. Cut a turkey beak and turkey legs out of yellow paper, and cut a turkey wattle out of red paper.

4. Glue the beak, legs, and wattle onto the puppet.

For More Fun

• Use your Turkey Puppet as you sing the turkey songs on pages 22 and 23.

• Make two Turkey Puppets and put on a Thanksgiving turkey play for your family and friends.

You Will Need

brown paper • felt-tip markers • scissors • yellow paper • red paper • glue

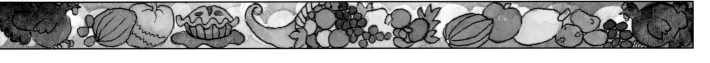

Native-American Counting Game

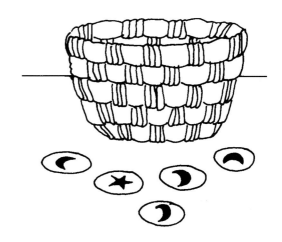

Making the Game

1. Cut five circle shapes out of cardboard.

2. Paint a half-moon shape on one side of four circles.

3. Paint a star shape on one side of the fifth circle.

4. When the paint has dried, place the circles in a basket.

Playing the Game

1. Choose a player to be the score-keeper and give him or her a pencil and a piece of paper.

2. Let each player shake the basket and then count out loud the number of shapes that turn face up.

3. The score-keeper should record the number and kind of shapes that turn face up after each player's turn.

4. After everyone has had a turn, count the points. Each moon shape is one point, and the star shape is two points. The player with the highest number of points is the winner.

For More Fun

• To make the game pieces the way Native Americans did, collect five plum pits and let them dry. Paint the half-moons and star on the dried plum pits.

You Will Need

cardboard • scissors • paint
• a paintbrush • a shallow basket • a pencil • a piece of writing paper

Graham-Cracker Turkeys

These may be the yummiest turkeys you'll eat this Thanksgiving!

1. Stir flours, baking soda, and salt together in a large bowl.

2. Ask an adult to help you mix apple-juice concentrate, vegetable oil, banana, vanilla, and cinnamon in a blender.

You Will Need

1 cup graham flour

1 cup whole-wheat flour

½ teaspoon baking soda

½ teaspoon salt

¼ cup apple-juice concentrate

¼ cup vegetable oil

1 banana, sliced

1 teaspoon vanilla

1 teaspoon cinnamon

3. Stir together the dry mixture and the wet mixture.

4. Using a rolling pin, roll the dough on a floured surface until it is ½-inch thick.

5. Cut the dough with a turkey-shaped cookie cutter.

6. Make feathers by using a fork to poke holes in the tail.

7. Poke one hole to make an eye.

8. Place the turkeys on a baking sheet and bake for 8 minutes at 350°F. Makes 2 to 3 dozen cookies, depending on the size of your cookie cutter.

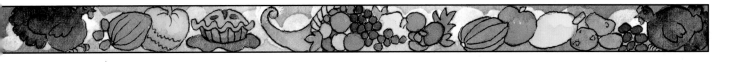

Sweet-Potato Pudding

You Will Need

¼ cup apple-juice
   concentrate

2 cups cooked sweet
   potatoes

⅓ cup orange juice

1 banana, sliced

1 teaspoon cinnamon

2 eggs

Try this nutritious, sugarless treat — you'll be in for a big surprise!

1. Ask an adult to help you mix all ingredients together in a blender.

2. Pour the mixture into a greased baking dish.

3. Bake for 40 minutes at 350°F. Makes 8 to 10 servings.

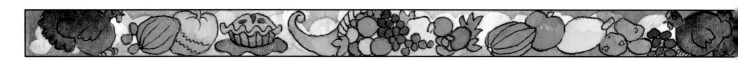

A Note to Parents and Teachers

The activities in this book have been written so that children in first, second and third grade can follow most of the directions with minimal adult help.

The activities are also appropriate for 3- to 5-year-old children, who can easily do the suggested activities with your help.

You may also wish to extend the learning opportunities in this book by discussing family gatherings and how we tell and show people that we love them.

Family gatherings are a great time to take advantage of natural learning opportunities. Children can start learning the concept of sets and patterns when they help set the table. Encourage your children to name the colors of fruits found in a fruit basket. Let your children learn about one-to-one correspondance as they match napkins or chairs to people. Teach your children the names and relationships of family members.

Children learn so much better when they can express their ideas and feelings through age-appropriate activities. We know you'll enjoy seeing your children's eyes light up when you extend a story with related activities.

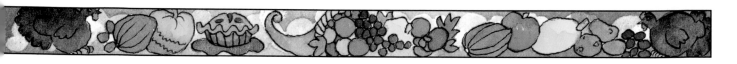

Huff and Puff's Thanksgiving

Sung to: "Up on the Housetop"

Up in the sky on Thanksgiving Day
Came some clouds from far away.
They came to be with Huff and Puff
And the rest of the family of Uff's.

Gruff and Muff,
Stuff and Fluff,
Ruff and Tuff,
Baby Buff.

They came with food for everyone,
They came with games to have some fun.

When they had eaten and the dishes were done,
They sat and watched the setting sun.
Then they sang and played some games,
Calling each other by their names,

Gruff and Muff,
Stuff and Fluff,
Ruff and Tuff,
Baby Buff.

Thanksgiving Day — a time to share
And to let your loved ones know you care.

Jean Warren